5

Come join Prune, Prosper and Fido.
To follow them in their adventure,
unfold the pull-out picture.

Investigate With Prune and Prosper

At the Beach

I am written by Michel Laporte

I am drawn by Alexandra Poulot

BARRON'S
New York • London • Toronto • Sydney

Hurray for vacation!
Prune, Prosper and Fido are at the beach.
Suddenly, Prune jumps up. "Prosper, did you
see the Sandkin there?
It just leaped off the sand castle and
went off toward the refreshment stand!"
"The Sandkins are here? Oh! my goodness," says Prosper.
"We have to find them or we won't have any peace!"

Prosper has reason to worry.
The Sandkins are terrible jokers!
Though they are usually about as large as chicks, they can
also make themselves as small as fleas.
They have a talent for hiding and they take
advantage of it by playing the most mischievous tricks!
Fortunately, they're not really mean, and
they are always willing to repair the damage
they have caused . . . but you have to find them!

"Come on, Prune, Fido, we have to look for them!
Let's check at the refreshment stand first."

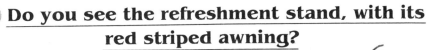

**Do you see the refreshment stand, with its
red striped awning?**

"What a mess here! Everything is upside down!
Our Sandkin has definitely been here."
"Look, he's still there, I see him!" says Prune.

Do you see him?
(He's hiding inside one of the bottles.)

There he is. Prune has caught him.
But the waiter at the refreshment stand is not happy!
"Where is the tray that I prepared—
and the bottle of soda, a glass and a straw?"
"It wasn't me, it wasn't me," sobs the Sandkin.

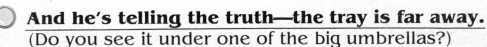

And he's telling the truth—the tray is far away.
(Do you see it under one of the big umbrellas?)

"My name is Sandette," says the small animal. "You have proved my innocence, so I'll help you straighten up the refreshment stand."

But there's still one object that doesn't belong in the refreshment stand. Do you see it?

"Did you come here all alone?" Prosper asks the Sandkin.
"No, my mother is hiding behind Cabin 1.
Will you take me there?"

 Can you find this cabin?

"Next, you can try to find my little brother.
He is near the fisherman."
"But, how many beside you are on this beach?" asks Prune.
"That's simple—just count the sunglasses and you'll know."

 **Can you find four pairs of sunglasses?**

This fisherman is well equipped to catch fish.
"But, look!" says Prune. "I see something that
doesn't look like a fishing lure! That must be our Sandkin!"

Do you see it?

The fisherman is grumpy. His net has disappeared.
"One of those little creatures has played a trick on me!"
"It wasn't me, it wasn't me!" says the Sandkin.
"He's right", says Prosper. "I found your net!"

 **A little girl has the net.
Do you see where it is?**

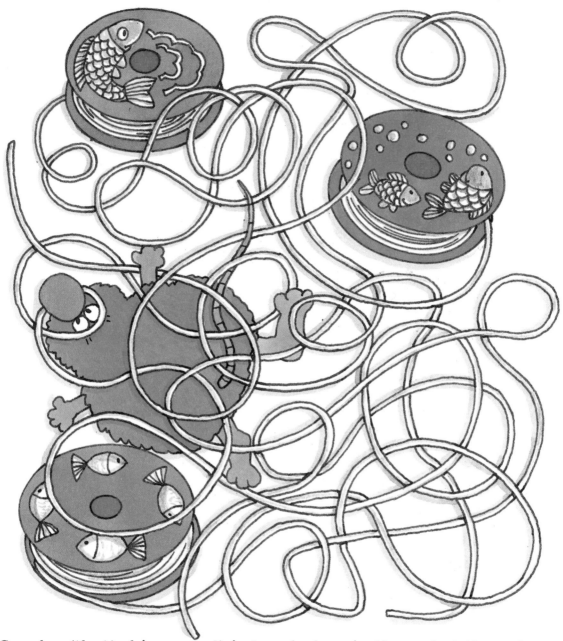

Sandor (that's his name!) is tangled up in the nylon thread.
"Help! Help me to get out of here,
and I will tell you where my sister Sanderella is!"

**To get Sandor out of there,
trace the thread of each spool.**

"Oh! Take me back to my mother.
Now she's behind the blue cabin."

 What is the number of the blue cabin?

Sandor likes Fido so much that he wants to adopt him.
"Let's go," says Sandra, his mother,
pulling him as hard as she can.
"Now tell our friends where Sanderella is hidden!"
"She's in the radio, near the baby on the towel," says Sandor.

Can you find the radio?
Actually, radios are forbidden on the beach!

**If the lifeguard comes,
how many fines would he give to people with radios?**

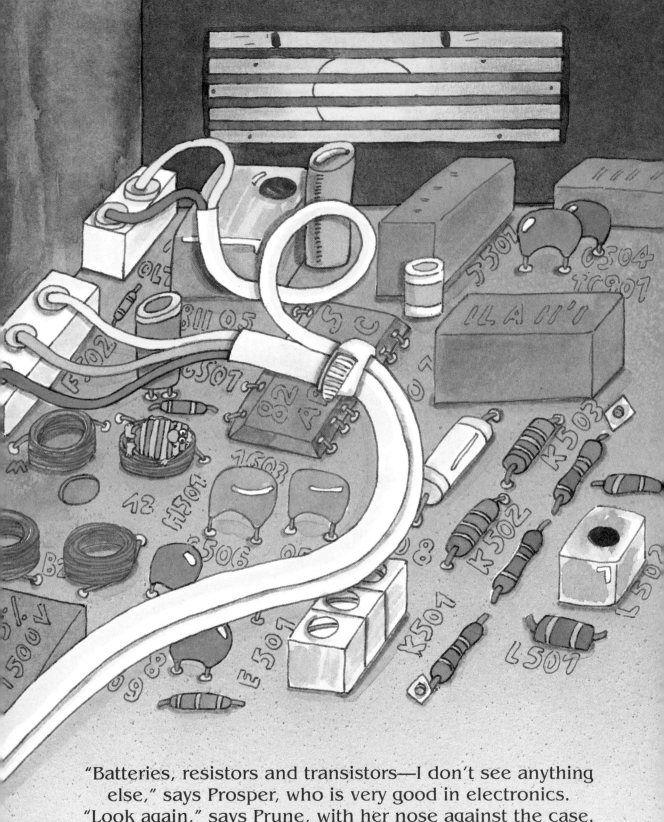

"Batteries, resistors and transistors—I don't see anything else," says Prosper, who is very good in electronics. "Look again," says Prune, with her nose against the case. "I see her!"

You see her, too, don't you?

Whoops! With a leap, Sanderella jumps out of the radio.
"There, Prosper. Now she is hiding in the sand castle!"

Yes, but which sand castle?
The one with round towers?
Or the one with square towers?

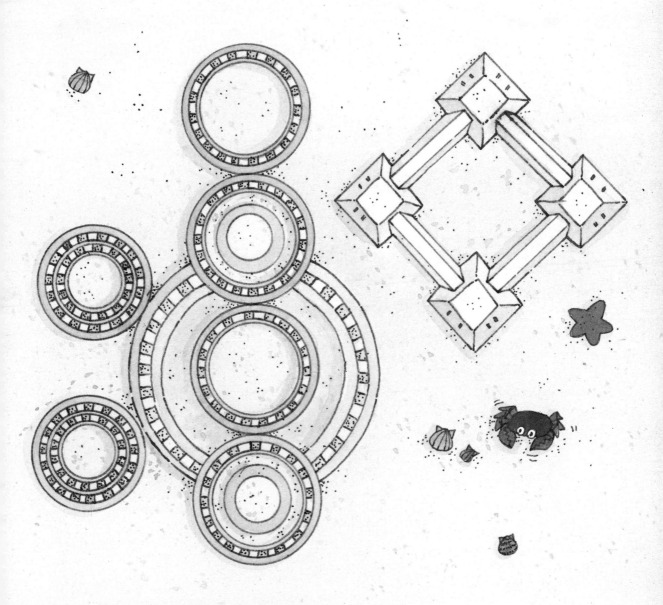

 It is simple. Sanderella is in the one
near the crying baby.

"Waah, waah!" cries the baby.
Someone has taken his red headphones.
"It wasn't me! It wasn't me!" protests Sanderella.
But Fido has found the real thief.

Do you see who has the red headphones?
Can you find six dogs on the beach?

Now Sanderella has been returned to her mother.
"Good! Only one more, and we can go swimming!" says Prune.
Yes, only one. Sandilla is hidden inside the big lady's purse—
the lady with the three children.
Do you see her?
(Her smallest daughter is dragging a doll behind her.)

"Whoof! Whoof!" Fido sticks his nose into the big purse.
He smells the Sandkin there!

**Fido has found Sandilla.
Do you see where she is hiding?**

"How awful!" screams the big lady. "My suntan lotion
has disappeared! I'm sure that the Sandkin took it!"
"It wasn't me, it wasn't me!" says Sandilla.
That's true—this lady is very absent-minded. She has
forgotten that she lent her bottle of lotion to her friend
in the blue and green striped bathing suit!

 Do you see where she is?

Sandilla did not take the bottle.
But she did tear up all the pictures in the lady's purse.

**Can you match up the pieces? How many
pictures are there?**

Before going home to Sandytown
the Sandkins plant candy on the beach
to apologize for their tricks.

**Can you tell how many candies are green and how
many are red?**

Sandra has finally found all her children—
Sandette, Sandor, Sanderella, and Sandilla.
Hurray for Prune, Prosper and Fido
"Bye, Bye, Sandkins!"
"So long! Come see us in Sandytown!"

They will go. They've promised. But, in the meantime . . .